Book design by Nicole Eckenrode.
Typeset in Café Mimi and Avenir.
Printed in Belgium
0-8118-2664-3

Library of Congress Cataloging-in-Publication Data available.

Distributed in Canada by Raincoast Books
8680 Cambie Street, Vancouver, British Columbia V6P 6M9

10 9 8 7 6 5 4 3 2 1

Chronicle Books
85 Second Street, San Francisco, California 94105

www.chroniclebooks.com/Kids

Squiggle's Tale

André Dahan

chronicle books·san francisco

Squiggle was so excited!
He was spending the summer in Paris
with his cousins, Snook and Puddin.

He promised his parents he would be good and sent
this letter to show them he was keeping his word.

Dear Mom and Dad,

Yesterday we went to Luxembourg Park. It was great!
There was a huge fountain in the middle of the park.
We dipped our toes in just a tiny bit. It felt really good.

When we were done
looking at the fountain,
we decided to sit on the
grass while our toes dried.

While we were resting we noticed a statue.
It was so tall that we couldn't see it very well.
We stood on our tippy toes to get a better look.

From the statue we spied a balloon stand, so we
ran over and bought some pretty colored balloons.
Lots of friendly people waved to us from the
balconies of a nearby palace!
Wasn't that nice?

The people here are very friendly.
I shared my balloons with some
people playing cards. They were happy
to show me how to play their game.

The most fun we had was riding on the ponies.
Did you know that ponies understand
any language?
When I said "giddy-up" my pony
started to run.

A man with a cap came chasing after us
shouting, "the money, the money!"
I looked down but I didn't see any money.

We rode around the carousel.
That man with the cap raced all the way around
with us, and he wasn't even on a horse!
Imagine that!

The ponies had never been to a
puppet show, so we brought them
to see "The Three Little Pigs."

The man in the cap came too.
Everyone had a really
good time.

After the show, we decided to have a treat.
We got a little bit of cotton candy—but not too much.
We didn't want to spoil our appetites for dinner.

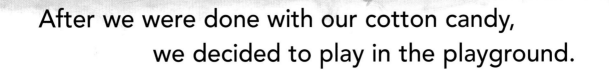

After we were done with our cotton candy,
we decided to play in the playground.

We slid down the slide, swung on the swings,
and made lots of new friends

Afterwards, we saw some birds
     that had landed on a big lawn.

We stayed quiet and still so
they wouldn't be frightened away.

At one end of the lawn there was a bandstand. We went over
to watch the musicians playing and ran right into a girl named Lucie.

She shared her hula hoop with us and offered us cookies.

Aunt Agatha asked us not to eat too many sweets,
so we said, "No thank you."

Then, Lucie had a great idea:
We could help rake leaves!

Then, we took a nice, quiet stroll through
the park until it was closing time!

We said goodbye to Lucie.

On the way out of the park, we decided we should
bring something special home for Auntie Agatha. It was
so nice that the gardener left some flowers for us to pick.

So, you see, I'm being good. I wish you were here.
Hugs and kisses. Love, Squiggle